WARWICK GOBLE

Princess
Stories

~

Princess Stories

A CLASSIC ILLUSTRATED EDITION

~

Compiled by Cooper Edens

chronicle books·san francisco

In memory of Princess Di
— *C. E.*

Book design by Jessica Dacher.
Typeset in Mrs. Eaves and Requiem.
Manufactured in China.

Library of Congress Cataloging-in-Publication Data available.

Distributed in Canada by Raincoast Books
9050 Shaughnessy Street, Vancouver, British Columbia V6P 6E5

10 9 8 7 6 5 4 3 2 1

Chronicle Books LLC
85 Second Street, San Francisco, California 94105

www.chroniclekids.com

~ Preface ~

There is an abundance of folklore available to humankind. Each culture's account of these tales—indeed each individual retelling—is a combination of preexisting symbols that have appeared in various forms around the world. The stories that have survived are those that fuse these symbols most adroitly.

Gathering the stories *Cinderella* (first published in 1697), *The Frog Prince* (1812), *The Little Mermaid* (1836), *The Princess and the Pea* (1836), *Rapunzel* (1812), *Sleeping Beauty* (1696), *Snow White and the Seven Dwarfs* (1812), and *Beauty and the Beast* (1756) into one volume combines some of the most astonishing symbolism in a literature. From Cinderella's glass slipper and midnight warning to Sleeping Beauty's spindle and hundred-year spell to the living mirror and glass coffin in *Snow White,* we find evidence of our fascination with the arcane through the centuries.

But even these symbols are faint in comparison to what I believe to be these princesses' common origin and shared purpose. The stories of eight girls supernaturally involved in becoming princesses are, in fact, one and the same story—a story that clearly represents to us that evil cannot absolutely destroy what is real and good.

There is a romantic idea that folktales come from the people. They don't. Folktales come from teachers, shamans, and visionaries who translate what they see and hear into ritual forms. Other visionaries then reinvent these forms and breathe new life into them as time passes.

Such has been the destiny of these eight princesses. Beginning with Cinderella, who entered folklore over a thousand years ago in China, their stories spread around the world, were graced by the master illustrators Rackham, Dulac, Sowerby, Nielsen, Robinson, and Jesse Wilcox Smith, and were eventually glorified on film by Walt Disney.

Now as we begin a new century there is no argument: These eight princesses are powerful, if not indomitable. They exist on their own, free from their creators, and rich in the promise to always exist and never have the virtue they symbolize transcended.

— Cooper Edens

~ Table of Contents ~

Cinderella..12

The Frog Prince..40

The Little Mermaid...46

The Princess and the Pea..72

Rapunzel..76

Sleeping Beauty..80

Snow White and the Seven Dwarfs...........................96

Beauty and the Beast..120

Acknowledgments..130

CHAPTER I

Cinderella

by Charles Perrault

here was once an honest gentleman who took for his second wife the most strict and most disagreeable lady in the whole country. She had two daughters exactly like herself. He, too, had a daughter — the loveliest girl ever known.

The wedding was no sooner over than the stepmother began to be very harsh and unkind toward this young girl, whose gentle and loving disposition caused the behavior of her own daughters to appear even more detestable than before. She gave her all the hard work of the house, compelling her to wash the floors and staircases, to dust the bedrooms, and scrub the pots and kettles.

While her stepsisters occupied beautiful rooms, with feather beds and pillows, the softest and most luxurious that money could buy, and with mirrors in which they could see themselves from head to foot, this poor young girl was sent to sleep in an attic, on an old straw mattress, with only one chair and not a looking glass in the room.

She suffered all in silence, not daring to complain to her father, who was entirely ruled by his new wife. When her daily work was done, she would sit for warmth in a corner of the chimney, among the cinders; and for this reason, and to show how much they despised her, the unkind stepsisters gave her the name of Cinderella.

But with her faded woolen dress and ribbonless hair, Cinderella looked a thousand times lovelier than her two wicked stepsisters did when they wore their brightest silks and a whole rainbow of ribbons in their hair.

It happened that the king's son gave a series of grand balls, to which were invited all the rank and fashion of the country, and among the rest the two stepsisters. They were very proud and happy, and occupied their whole time in deciding what they should wear. This was a source of new trouble to Cinderella, whose duty it was to do all their sewing and ironing, to starch and plait their fine linen, laces, and ruffles, and who never could please them, however much she tried.

The stepsisters gave themselves much loftier airs than before; and it seemed as if they would never cease discussing how they should be dressed. "I," said the elder, "shall wear my red velvet gown and my trimmings of English lace."

"Well!" said the younger, "I shall put on my ordinary silk petticoat, but I shall adorn it with an upper skirt of flowered brocade, and have my pearl and diamond coronet, which is a great deal finer than anything of yours." Here the elder sister grew angry, and the dispute began to run so high that Cinderella, who was known to have excellent taste, was called upon to decide between them. She gave them the best advice she could, and gently and submissively offered to dress them herself.

The important evening came, and she exercised all her skill in adorning the two young ladies. While she was combing out the elder's hair, this ill-natured girl said sharply, "Cinderella, do you not wish you were going to the ball?"

"Ah, madam"—they obliged her always to say madam—"you are only mocking me; it is not my fortune to have any such pleasure."

"Yes, you are right," said the other sister, tossing her head, "people would only laugh to see a little cinder-wench at a ball." After this, any other girl would have dressed the hair all awry, but Cinderella was good, and dressed it perfectly even and smooth and as pretty as she could.

So anxious were the two sisters to improve their figures, they had scarcely eaten for three days, and had broken a dozen stay-laces a day in trying to make themselves slender; but tonight they broke a dozen more, and lost their tempers over and over again before Cinderella had them dressed for the ball. When at last the happy moment arrived she followed them to the courtyard, and when the stepsisters whirled away, she kept her eyes fixed on the carriage until it disappeared. Then Cinderella went back to her usual seat in the chimney corner, and sat down by the kitchen fire and cried.

Suddenly she heard a voice say, "What is the matter, my poor child?" And to her astonishment, Cinderella saw a mystical lady with a long ebony wand appear from out of nowhere.

"Did nobody ever tell you that you had a fairy godmother?" asked the lady.

"When I was a tiny child someone did," said Cinderella, "but I thought you had forgotten me."

"No, indeed," declared the fairy. "I never forget, but I choose my own time to show that I remember. Now tell me, child, what are you crying about?"

"Oh, I wish. . . I wish. . ." Her sobs stopped her.

"You wish to go to the ball; isn't it so?" Cinderella nodded. "Well then, be a good girl, and you shall go. First lead me out into the garden and we shall pick the largest pumpkin we can find."

Cinderella did not understand what this had to do with going to the ball, but being obliging, she escorted her fairy godmother to the garden. Then the fairy chose the finest pumpkin of all and scooped it hollow. "That is good as far as it goes," said the fairy, "but it won't go far without horses!

"Now," said the fairy, "fetch me the mousetrap out of the pantry, my dear." Cinderella ran quickly and was delighted to find six of the whitest, sleekest mice caught in the trap. There they were, poking their little noses through the bars and trying to get out. And how they did squeal! Cinderella took care that not one of them should escape, as she opened the trap in triumph before her fairy godmother.

"Well, my child," said the fairy, "this is a fine turnout truly. But there are the finishing touches yet to be put on. Go and check behind the firewood and you will find a large black rat in the rattrap."

Further puzzled, Cinderella ran with all haste, and soon returned bearing the trap, which had in it a rat of the very best quality.

And this was not all. "Bring me six green lizards," said the fairy godmother. "You will find them behind the watering pot in the garden." Once more Cinderella did not question her godmother but did as she was told.

"Perfect," said the fairy. "Now shut your eyes while I count to seven." Cinderella did, and as her fairy godmother counted, Cinderella heard some strange noises. First, she heard the tapping of the long ebony wand and then footsteps and the clattering of hoofs.

When Cinderella finally opened her eyes, she found, first in miniature — and then all at once in full size — a magnificent gold coach drawn by six white horses with arching necks, shining manes, and long elegant tails, driven by a fat coachman with the finest whiskers imaginable and attended by six footmen all in splendid liveries of green and gold. "There, Cinderella!" exclaimed her fairy godmother, gazing with pride upon the equipage. "Could anything be finer than that? Jump in, and be off."

Cinderella looked at her shabby clothes, contrasting them with the splendor of the carriage, and shook her head sadly. The fairy godmother understood at once and said, "Oh, I see! You think that dress is hardly fit to wear to a ball. Well, we can easily remedy that. My dressmaker is wonderfully skillful and will fit you out in short order." Saying this, she touched Cinderella with her wand, and immediately the threadbare clothes fell off the young girl, and she stood arrayed in a beautiful jacket that shone like cloth of gold and her ragged woolen petticoat lengthened into a gown of sweeping satin.

Jewels sparkled here and there — on her hands, at her throat, and on her waist — and to crown all, the fairy brought a pair of lovely silken slippers that shone with diamonds for Cinderella to put on.

The godmother paused awhile to admire Cinderella in her new attire, and then she said, "I have but one warning to give you, my child. Be certain to leave the ballroom before twelve o'clock, for if you remain one instant beyond that time, your carriage will become a pumpkin, your coachman, a rat, your horses, mice, and your footmen, lizards. Your beautiful dress, too, will vanish away, leaving you in the shabby clothes of a kitchen drudge."

Cinderella, in a flutter of excitement and eager to be off, promised all her fairy godmother wished. Her promise was without fear, because her heart was so full of joy, and away dashed the carriage for the ball.

A few moments later, the coach arrived in the royal courtyard, the door was flung open, and Cinderella alighted. As she walked slowly up the richly carpeted staircase, there was a murmur of admiration. The prince was dancing a minuet with a duchess of the court, when suddenly the music stopped and all the dancers turned toward the entrance of the ballroom. Cinderella had arrived, and her beauty, together with her dazzling gown, had created such a stir that for a moment the fiddlers could not fiddle and the dancers could not dance. There was a long, still hush, then confused whispers all over the room: "Here she comes!" "Oh! How beautiful!"

As soon as the band struck up again, the prince left the duchess and went to greet the mysterious guest. "Never," said he to himself, "have I seen anyone so lovely!" And he offered Cinderella his hand.

The young prince led her with the utmost courtesy through the assembled guests, who stood aside to let her pass, whispering to one another, "Oh, how enchanting she is!" It might have turned the head of anyone but poor Cinderella, who was so used to being despised, but she took it all as if it were something happening in a fairy tale.

Her triumph was complete; even the old king said to the queen that never since Her Majesty's young days had he seen so charming a person. All the court ladies scanned her eagerly, clothes and all, and determined to have theirs made the next day of exactly the same pattern, if they could but get artists skillful enough, and purchase the same extraordinary material. The evening passed away in a dream of delight, Cinderella dancing with no one but the handsome young prince. So exquisitely graceful were Cinderella's movements that she and the prince were the only couple dancing, with everybody else looking on.

At the supper, which was most sumptuously served, the young prince had no appetite, but kept his eyes fixed tenderly on his unknown visitor, who

had taken a seat by the side of her naughty stepsisters and was giving them a share of all the delicacies that the prince passed to her. The two sisters could not recognize their ragged little sister in the graceful lady to whom the prince paid so much attention, and felt quite pleased and flattered when she addressed a few words to them.

When their merriment was at its highest, the clock struck a quarter to twelve. Startled, Cinderella remembered her fairy godmother's warning and said that, alas, she must now leave. The guests rose from the table and crowded in the hall to see her go.

While the stepsisters stood on the marble staircase, waving their handkerchiefs, the prince, himself, helped her into the coach. So fascinated was the prince with Cinderella that he then requested his attendants to follow her and learn of her destination. But her white horses were too fast and the prince's pages could not keep up with the carriage, so the identity of the princess remained a mystery.

Once home she found her fairy godmother, who smiled approval. When Cinderella asked her permission to go to the second ball the following night, the fairy replied, "Why yes, of course, but this time, my child, you must go to the garden alone, and near your mother's grave and under the hazel tree whisper these words:

"Rustle and shake yourself, dear tree,
And silver and gold throw down to me."

Before Cinderella could ask the fairy why she should do this, the two terrible stepsisters were heard knocking at the gate, and the fairy godmother and Cinderella's magic clothes vanished, leaving her sitting in the chimney corner, rubbing her eyes and pretending to be very sleepy. "Oh! How late you are!" she yawned, rubbing her eyes and stretching herself as though she had just woken up.

"Ah!" cried the eldest sister spitefully. "You would not have been so sleepy, if you had been with us. It was the most delightful ball, and there was present the most lovely princess we ever saw, who was so exceedingly polite to us both."

"Was she?" said Cinderella indifferently. "And whom might she be?"

"Nobody knows, though everybody would give their eyes to know, especially the king's son, who was greatly distressed at her leaving so suddenly, and would give all the world to find out where she came from."

"Indeed!" replied Cinderella, a little more interested. "I should like to see her." Then she tuned to the elder sister and said, "Madame, will you not let me go tomorrow, and lend me your yellow gown that you wear on Sundays?"

"What, lend my yellow gown to a cinder-wench! I am not so mad as that!"

"Oh the idea!" the other sister screamed. "A kitchen-hussy like you! What next will you think of?" And they walked away, holding their grotesque and sneering noses high up in the air.

The next night, when the festival was renewed and her stepsisters had set out again, Cinderella followed her godmother's advice and went to the garden, and near her mother's grave and under the hazel tree whispered the words the fairy had told her:

> "Rustle and shake yourself, dear tree,
> And silver and gold throw down on me."

Instantly a flock of mysterious birds threw down an even more splendid dress and this time a pair of the smallest and prettiest slippers that had ever been seen — they were made of glass, but were soft as silk, and fitted her exactly.

The gown and the slippers Cinderella put on in great haste and then suddenly she discovered her godmother standing beside her, waiting with the pumpkin coach. And she just had time to look out the carriage's window as it set off for the ball to hear her fairy godmother's voice: "Now, remember twelve o'clock" were her parting words; and Cinderella thought she certainly should remember.

When Cinderella appeared at the ball, everyone was even more astonished at her beauty. This time instead of ceasing to play when she entered the ballroom, the fiddlers struck up the merriest tune and the prince walked straight up to her and kissed her hand.

The prince's attentions to her were greater even than on the first evening, and in the delight of listening to his pleasant conversation, time slipped by unperceived. The prince told Cinderella he would dance with no one else, and even would not let go of her hand, so that when anyone else asked her to dance, he said, "She is my partner."

Cinderella's stepsisters did not know her at all but took her for some foreign princess, as she looked so wonderful dancing in her little glass slippers; for of Cinderella they thought not but that she was sitting at home picking beans out of ashes.

The minutes flew even more quickly than they had the night before, and in the embrace of the prince's arms, as they enjoyed dance after dance, Cinderella forgot all about her fairy godmother's warning.

The prince led Cinderella out to the balcony so that she might admire the palace garden. While she was sitting beside him in a lovely alcove and looking at the moon from under a bower of orange blossoms, she heard the great bronze bell begin to toll midnight from the distant belfry of the cathedral.

Millicent Sowerby.

Cinderella gave a cry of alarm, gathered up her magical gown, and fled away as lightly as a deer.

She rushed through the ballroom and flew down the marble stairway.

The prince ran after Cinderella as she heard the clock toll nine, ten, eleven . . .

At the stroke of twelve, as Cinderella reached the bottom of the stairway, she watched in awe and dismay as her carriage became a pumpkin, her coachman, a rat, her horses, mice, and her footmen, lizards. Her beautiful dress, too, vanished away, leaving her in the shabby clothes of a kitchen drudge.

When the prince reached the gateway of the palace, Cinderella had disappeared from sight. Indeed, he missed his lovely princess altogether and only saw running out of the palace grounds a little dirty lass whom he had never beheld before, and of whom he certainly would never have taken the least notice. The prince asked the sentinel on guard if he had seen a princess in a golden gown drive away in a golden coach. The sentinel shook his head. He did not even think to mention the little ragged girl who had sped up the road on foot a minute before.

Puzzled, the prince returned to the balcony to see if, by any chance, he could catch a gleam of the golden carriage on the road far below. But no such coach was to be seen, and so, sadly, the prince turned away. As he did, he saw a gleam of crystal at his feet. It was one of the glass slippers, which had fallen off in Cinderella's flight. The prince picked it up and would not part with it.

Poor Cinderella arrived at home frightened and out of breath, with no carriage, no horses, no coachman, no footmen—and all her old clothes back again. She had none of her finery now, except the other glass slipper. When the stepsisters returned, they were full of this strange adventure: how the beautiful lady had appeared at the ball more beautiful than ever and enchanted everyone who looked at her; and how as the clock was striking twelve, she had suddenly risen up and fled from the garden and through the ballroom, disappearing no one

knew how or where, and dropping one of her glass slippers behind her in her flight. "The prince picked it up and has been looking at it and kissing it ever since. Everybody says he is madly in love with her," said the eldest sister, in a romantic tone.

Cinderella listened in silence, turning her face to the kitchen fire, and perhaps it was that which made her look so rosy; but nobody ever noticed or admired her at home, so it did not signify, and the next morning she went to her weary work again just as before.

The king's son had remained inconsolable, though he had chanced to pick up the little glass slipper, which he carried away in his pocket and was seen to take out continually, and look at affectionately, with the air of a man very much in love; in fact, from his behavior during the remainder of the evening, all the court and the royal family were sure that he was desperately in love with the wearer of the little glass slipper.

And so he was. For the next day three trumpeters stood atop the palace, proclaiming that the prince would marry the lady who could wear the little glass slipper:

"Alas, when she left the prince,
he sadly went apart;
The slipper she had lost, he found—
he clasped it to his heart;
And now this proclamation,
by means of heralds three:
The lady whom this slipper fits,
our royal bride shall be!"

A few days after, the whole kingdom was attracted by the sight of a herald going around with the little glass slipper in his hand, announcing, with a flourish of trumpets, that the king's son had ordered it to be fitted on the foot of every lady in the kingdom, and that he wished to marry the lady whom it fitted best, or to whom it and the fellow slipper belonged.

Great was the excitement of all the unmarried ladies in the kingdom. Wherever the herald stopped, hundreds of ladies came running, all eager to see if they could squeeze their feet into the little glass slipper. Princesses, duchesses, countesses, and simple gentlewomen all tried it on, but their feet were all much too large; and, besides, nobody could produce its fellow slipper, which lay all the time safely in the pocket of Cinderella's old woolen gown.

At last the herald came to the house of the mean stepsisters, and though they knew very well that neither of them was the beautiful princess, they tried hard to get their large clumsy feet into it, but could not. "May I see if it will fit me?" said Cinderella from the chimney corner.

"What, you?" cried the sisters, bursting into shouts of laughter; but Cinderella only smiled and put her foot on the herald's tasseled pillow. Her

sisters could not prevent her, since the command was that every maiden in the kingdom should try on the slipper, in order that no chance might be left untried, for the prince was nearly breaking his heart; and his father and mother were afraid that he would actually die for love of the beautiful unknown lady.

So the herald bade Cinderella to place her foot on a stool in the kitchen, and he himself put the slipper on her pretty little foot. It fitted exactly.

The two sisters bit their lips in envy and vexation—and they nearly fainted when Cinderella put her hand into her pocket and brought out the other slipper, which she also put on, and stood up. With the touch of the magic shoes, all her dress was changed likewise. No longer was she the poor, despised cinder-wench, but now the beautiful lady the king's son loved.

Then the stepsisters recognized that Cinderella was the amazing princess whom they had seen at the ball, and throwing themselves on their knees, asked her to forgive them the very many unkind things they had said and done to her. She lifted them up, kissed them affectionately, and said she only wanted them to love her now.

Cinderella was summoned outside the house, where the king and queen had sent their own royal carriage to bring her to the prince. She was at once taken to the palace, where the prince watched her step from the coach and welcomed her with open heart. The prince thought Cinderella more lovely and lovable than ever, and insisted upon marrying her immediately.

After the glorious wedding, Cinderella never went home again, but she called her two sisters to the palace and married them shortly after to two gentlemen of the court. Wishing that for their son and his princess all happy things might come to pass, the king and queen and all the court threw for luck old slippers (not of glass) into the air as they departed for their kingdom tour. And the prince and his princess became — after many loving years — a noble king and queen of great historic fame.

CHAPTER 2

The Frog Prince
by The Brothers Grimm

One fine evening, a young princess sat by the side of a cool spring of water. She had a golden ball in her hand and she amused herself by tossing it into the air and catching it as it fell. After a time she threw it up so high that when she stretched out her hand to catch it, the ball bounded away and rolled along, till at last it fell into the spring.

The princess looked into the spring, but it was deep, so deep that she could not see the bottom of it. Then she began to cry and said, "Alas! If I could only get my ball again, I would give all my fine clothes and jewels and everything that I have in the world."

While she was crying, a frog poked its head out of the water and said, "Princess, why do you weep so bitterly?"

"Alas!" said she, "what can you do for me, you ugly frog? My golden ball has fallen into the spring."

The frog said, "I want not your pearls and jewels and fine clothes, but if you will love me and let me live with you and eat from your little golden plate and sleep upon your little bed, I will bring you your ball."

"What nonsense!" thought the princess. "He can never get out of the spring. However, he may be able to get my ball for me, and therefore I will promise him what he asks." So she said to the frog, "If you will bring me my ball, I promise to do all you ask." Then the frog dove deep under the water.

After a little while, he came up again with the ball in his mouth. As soon as the young princess saw her ball, she ran to pick it up, and was so overjoyed to have it in her hand again that she never even thought of the frog but ran home with the ball as fast as she could. The frog called after her, "Stay, Princess, and take me with you as you promised." But the princess did not stop to hear a word.

The next day, just as the princess had sat down to dinner, she heard a strange noise, *tap-tap-tap,* as if someone were coming up the marble staircase. Then someone knocked gently at the door.

The princess ran to the door and opened it, and there she saw the frog. She was terribly frightened, and, shutting the door as fast as she could, she returned to her seat. The king, her father, asked her what had frightened her. "There is a nasty frog at the door," she said, "who lifted my ball out of the spring yesterday. I promised him that he should live with me here, thinking that he could never get out of the spring, but there he is at the door and wants to come in!" While she was speaking, the frog knocked again at the door.

The king said to the young princess, "As you have made a promise, you must keep it. Go and let him in." She did so, and the frog hopped into the room and came up close to the table.

"Pray lift me upon a chair," said he to the princess, "and let me sit next to you." As soon as she had done this, the frog said, "Put your plate closer to me that I may eat out of it." This she did, and when he had eaten as much as he could, he said, "Now I am tired. Carry me upstairs and put me into your little bed." So the princess took him up in her hand and put him upon the pillow of her own little bed, where he slept all night long.

As soon as it was light he jumped up, hopped downstairs, and went out of the house. "Now," thought the princess, "he is gone, and I shall be troubled with him no more."

But she was mistaken, for when night came again, she heard the same tapping at the door. When she opened it, the frog came in and slept upon her pillow as before until morning. The third night he did the same, but when the princess awoke the following morning, she was astonished to see, instead of a frog, a handsome prince standing at the foot of her bed.

He told her that he had been enchanted by an evil fairy, who had changed him into a frog, and he would have had to remain a frog unless a princess should take him out of the spring and let him sleep upon her bed for three nights.

"You have broken this cruel charm," said the prince, "and now I have nothing to wish for but that you should go with me into my father's kingdom, where I will marry you and love you as long as I live."

The young princess, you may be sure, was not long in giving her con-
sent, and as they spoke, a splendid carriage drove up. It was driven by eight
beautiful horses decked with plumes of feathers and a golden harness, and
behind rode the prince's servant, the faithful Henry, who had bewailed the
misfortune of his dear master so long and bitterly that his heart had well-nigh
burst. Then all set out full of joy for the prince's kingdom, where they arrived
safely and lived happily a great many years.

CHAPTER 3

The Little Mermaid

by Hans Christian Andersen

ar out at sea the water is as blue as the petals of the prettiest corn-flower and as clear as the purest glass. But it's very deep, deeper than any anchor can reach. Many church steeples would have to be piled up, one on top of the other, to reach from the bottom of the sea up to the surface. Down there live the sea people.

Now, you mustn't for a moment imagine that there's nothing but bare, white sand down there. Oh, no! The most wonderful trees and plants grow at the bottom of the sea. Their stalks and leaves bend so easily that they stir with the slightest movement of the water, as if they were alive. All the fish, large and small, glide between the branches, just as birds fly through the trees up here. Down in the deepest spot of all is the castle of the sea king. Its walls are built of coral, and the long, pointed windows are made of the clearest amber. The roof is formed of shells that open and close with the current. It's a pretty sight, for each shell has a dazzling pearl, any one of which would be a splendid orna-ment for a queen's crown.

The sea king had been a widower for some years, and his aged mother kept house for him. She was an intelligent woman, but proud when it came to her noble birth. That's why she wore twelve oysters on her tail, while everyone else of high rank had to settle for six. Otherwise she deserved great praise, for she was very devoted to her granddaughters, the little sea princesses. They were

six pretty children, but the youngest was the loveliest of them all. Her skin was as clear and delicate as a rose leaf. Her eyes were as blue as the deepest sea. But, like all the others, she had no feet and her body ended in a fish tail.

All day long the sea princesses played in the great halls of the castle, where flowers grew right out of the walls. The large amber windows were open, and the fish swam in, just as swallows fly into our homes when we open the windows. The fish glided right up to the princesses, fed from their hands, and waited to be patted.

Outside the castle there was a beautiful garden with trees of deep blue and fiery red. Each of the little princesses had her own plot in the garden, where she could dig and plant as she pleased. One arranged her flower bed in the shape of a whale; another thought it nicer to make hers look like the figure of a little mermaid; but the youngest made hers quite round like the sun, and she wanted nothing but flowers that shone red like it. She was a curious child, quiet and thoughtful. While her sisters decorated their gardens with the wonderful things they obtained from sunken ships, she would have nothing but rose-red flowers that were like the sun high above, and a beautiful marble statue. The statue was of a handsome boy, chiseled from pure white stone, and it had come down to the bottom of the sea after a shipwreck.

Nothing pleased the princess more than to hear about the world of humans above the sea. Her old grandmother had to tell her all she knew of the ships and towns, the people and the animals.

"When you are fifteen," the grandmother told the princesses, "we will let you rise to the surface and sit on the rocks in the moonlight while the great ships sail past. You will see both forests and towns."

None of the mermaids was more curious than the youngest, and she, who was so silent and thoughtful, also had the longest wait. Many a night she stood at the open window and gazed up through the dark blue waters, where the fish splash with their fins and tails. She could see the moon and the stars, even though their light was rather pale.

Through the water they looked much larger than they do to us. If a black cloud passed above her, she knew that it was either a whale swimming over her head or a vessel filled with passengers. These people never imagined that a pretty little mermaid was beneath them, stretching up her white arms toward the keel of the ship.

Before the approach of a storm, when they expected a shipwreck, the sisters would swim in front of the vessel and sing sweetly of the delights to be found in the depths of the sea. They told the sailors not to be afraid of sinking down to the bottom, but the sailors never understood their songs. They thought they were hearing the howling of the storm. Nor did they ever see any of the delights the mermaids promised, because if the ship sank, the men were drowned, and only as dead men did they reach the palace of the sea king.

When the sisters floated up, arm in arm, through the water in this way, their youngest sister would always stay back all alone, gazing after them. She would have cried, but mermaids have no tears and suffer even more than we do. "Oh, if only I were fifteen years old," she would say. "I know that I will love the world up there and all the people who live in it."

Then at last she turned fifteen. "Well, now you'll soon be off our hands," said the old dowager queen, her grandmother. "Come, let me dress you up like your other sisters," and she put a wreath of white lilies in her hair, and each flower petal was half a pearl. And the old woman ordered eight big oysters to nip tight onto the princess's tail to show her high rank.

"Ow! That hurts," said the little mermaid.

"Yes, beauty has its price," the grandmother replied. How the princess would have liked to shake off all this finery and put away the heavy wreath! The red flowers in her garden suited her much better, but she didn't dare make any changes.

"Farewell," she said as she rose through the water as lightly and clearly as a bubble moves to the surface. The sun had just set as she lifted her head above the waves, but the clouds were still tinted with crimson and gold. Up in the pale, pink sky the evening star shone clear and bright. The air was mild and fresh, and the sea dead calm. A large three-masted ship was drifting in the water, with only one sail hoisted because not a breath of wind was stirring. The sailors were lolling about in the rigging and on the yards. There was music and singing on board, and when it grew dark, a hundred lanterns were lit. With their many colors, it looked as if the flags of all nations were fluttering in the air.

The little mermaid swam right up to the porthole of the cabin, and every time a wave lifted her up she could see a crowd of well-dressed people through the clear glass. Among them was a young prince, the handsomest person there, with large dark eyes. He could not have been more than sixteen. It was his birthday, and that's why there was so much of a stir. When the young prince came out on the deck, where the sailors were dancing, more than a hundred rockets swished up into the sky and broke into a glitter, making the sky as bright as day.

The little mermaid was so startled that she dove down under the water. But she quickly popped her head out again. And look! It was just as if all the stars up in heaven were falling down on her. She had never seen fireworks. Great suns went spinning around, gorgeous fiery fishes swooped into the blue air, and all this glitter was reflected in the clear, calm waters below. The ship itself was so brightly illuminated that you could see not only everyone there but even the smallest piece of rope. How handsome the young prince looked as he shook hands with the sailors! He laughed and smiled as the music sounded through the lovely night air.

It grew late, but the little mermaid could not take her eyes off the ship or the handsome prince. The colored lanterns had been extinguished; the rockets no longer rose in the air; and the cannon had ceased firing. But the sea had become restless, and you could hear a moaning, grumbling sound beneath the waves. Still, the mermaid stayed in the water, rocking up and down so that she could look into the cabin. The ship gathered speed; one after another of its sails was unfurled. The waves rose higher, heavy clouds darkened the sky, and lightning flashed in the distance. A dreadful storm was brewing. So the sailors took in the sails, while the great ship rocked and scudded through the raging sea. The waves rose higher and higher until they were like huge black mountains, threatening to bring down the mast.

The little mermaid suddenly realized that the ship was in danger. She herself had to be careful of the beams and bits of wreckage drifting in the water. One moment it was so dark that she could not see a thing, but then a flash of lightning lit up everyone on board. Now it was every man for himself. She was looking for the young prince, and, just as the ship was being torn apart, she saw him disappear into the depths of the sea. For just a moment she was quite pleased, for she thought he would now live in her part of the world. But then she remembered that human beings could not live underwater and that only as a dead man could he come down to her father's palace. No, no, he must not die. So she swam in among the drifting beams and planks, oblivious to the danger of being crushed. She dove deep down and came right back up again among the waves, and at last she found the young prince. He could hardly swim any longer in the stormy sea. His limbs were failing him, his beautiful eyes were closed, and he would certainly have drowned if the little mermaid had not come to his rescue. She held his head above water and then let the waves carry her along with him.

By morning the storm had died down, and there was not a trace of the ship. The sun rose red and glowing up out of the water and seemed to bring color back into the prince's cheeks, but his eyes remained closed. The mermaid kissed his fine, high forehead and smoothed back his wet hair. He seemed to her like the marble statue in her little garden. She kissed him again and made a wish that he might live.

Soon the mermaid saw the mainland before her, with its lofty blue mountains covered with glittering white snow that looked like nestling swans. Near the coast were lovely green forests, and close by was a large building, whether it was a church or a convent she could not say. Lemon and orange trees were growing in the garden, and at the door there were tall palm trees. The sea formed a small bay at this point, and the water in it was quite still, though very deep. The mermaid swam with the handsome prince to the beach, which was covered with fine, white sand. There she placed him in the warm sunshine, making a pillow for his head with the sand.

Bells sounded in the large white building, and a number of young girls came through the garden. The little mermaid swam farther out from the shore, hiding behind some large boulders that rose out of the water. She covered her hair and chest with sea foam so that no one could see her. Then she watched to see who would come to help the poor prince.

Not much later a young girl came along. When she saw the prince lying on the sand, she seemed quite frightened, but only for a moment, and ran to get help from others. The mermaid saw the prince come back to life, and he smiled at everyone around him. But there was no smile for her, because he had no idea that she had rescued him. After he was taken away, she felt so miserable that she dove into the water and returned to her father's palace.

She had always been silent and thoughtful, but now more so than ever. Her sisters asked her what she had seen during her first visit to the surface, but she told them nothing. Many a morning and many an evening she rose up to the spot where she had left the prince. She saw the fruits in the garden ripen and watched as they were harvested. She saw the snow melt on the peaks. But she never saw the prince, and so she always returned home, filled with even greater sorrow than before. Her one comfort was sitting in her little garden, with her arms around the beautiful marble statue, which was so like the prince. She gave up tending her flowers, and they grew into a kind of wilderness out over the paths, twining their long stalks and leaves around the branches of the trees until the light was quite shut out.

At length she could keep it to herself no longer and told one of her sisters everything. The others learned about it soon afterward, but no one else, except a few other mermaids who did not breathe a word to anyone but their best friends. One of them was able to give her news about the prince. She, too, had seen the festival held on the ship and told the little mermaid about the prince and the location of his kingdom.

Now that the little mermaid knew where the prince lived, she spent many an evening and many a night at that spot. She swam much closer to the shore than any of the others dared. She even went up the narrow channel to reach the fine marble balcony that threw its long shadow across the water. Here she would sit and gaze at the young prince, who thought that he was completely alone in the bright moonlight.

Often in the evening the little mermaid saw him go out to sea in his splendid vessel, with flags hoisted, to the strains of music. She peeked out from among the green rushes, and when the wind caught her long silvery white veil and people saw it, they just fancied it was a swan, spreading its wings.

On many nights, when the fishermen were out at sea with their torches, she heard them praising the young prince, and their words made her even happier that she had saved his life the day he was drifting about half-dead on the waves. And she remembered how she had cradled his head on her chest and how lovingly she had kissed him. But he knew nothing about any of this and never even dreamed she existed.

The little mermaid grew more and more fond of human beings and longed deeply for their company. Their world seemed so much larger than her own. You see, they could fly across the ocean in ships and climb the steep mountains high above the clouds. And the lands they possessed, their woods and their fields, stretched far beyond where she could see. There was so much that she would have liked to know, and her sisters were not able to answer all her questions. And so she went to visit her old grandmother, who knew all about the upper world, as she so aptly called the countries above the sea.

"If human beings don't drown," asked the little mermaid, "can they go on living forever? Don't they die, as we do down here in the sea?"

"Yes, yes," replied the old woman. "They, too, must die, and their lifetime is even shorter than ours. We sometimes live to the age of three hundred, but when our life here comes to an end, we merely turn into foam on the water. We don't even have a grave down here among those we love. We lack an immortal soul, and we shall never have another life. We're like the green rush. Once it's been cut, it stops growing. But human beings have souls that live forever, even after their bodies have turned to dust.

"They rise up through the pure air until they reach the shining stars. Just as we come up out of the water and survey the lands of human beings, so they rise up to beautiful, unknown realms—regions we shall never see."

"Why can't we have an immortal soul?" the little mermaid asked mournfully. "I would gladly give all three hundred years I have to live to become a human being for just one day and to share in that heavenly world."

"You mustn't go worrying about that," said the grandmother. "We're much happier and better off than the human beings who live up there."

"So then I'm doomed to die and float like foam on the sea, never to hear the music of the waves or see the lovely flowers and the red sun. Isn't there anything at all I can do to win an immortal soul?"

"No," said the old woman. "Only if a human loved you so much that you meant more to him than father and mother. If he were to love you with all his heart and soul and let the priest place his right hand in yours as a promise to be faithful and true here and in all eternity—then his soul would glide into your body and you, too, would obtain a share of human happiness. He would give you a soul and yet keep his own. But that can never happen. Your fish tail, which we find so beautiful, looks repulsive to people on earth. They know so little about it that they really believe the two clumsy supports they call legs look nice."

The little mermaid sighed and looked mournfully at her fish tail. "We must be satisfied with what we have," said the old woman. "Let's dance and be joyful for the three hundred years we have to live—that's really quite time enough. After that we'll rest all the better and get our fill of sleep after we die. Tonight we are going to have a court ball."

That was something more splendid than anything we ever see on earth. The walls and ceiling of the great ballroom were made of thick, but transparent, crystal. Several hundred enormous shells, rose red and grass green, were ranged on either side, each with a blue flame that lit up the entire room and, by shining through the walls, also lit up the sea. Countless fish, large and small, could be seen swimming toward the crystal walls. The scales on some of them glowed with a purple-red brilliance, and on others like silver and gold. Through the middle of the ballroom flowed a broad stream, and in it mermen and mermaids were dancing to their own sweet song. No human beings have voices so lovely.

The little mermaid sang more sweetly than anyone else, and everyone applauded her. For a moment there was joy in her heart, for she knew that she had the most beautiful voice of anyone on land or in the sea. But then her thoughts turned to the world above her. She was unable to forget the handsome prince and her great sorrow that she lacked the immortal soul he had. So she crept out of her father's palace, and while everyone inside was singing and making merry, she sat grieving in her own little garden.

Suddenly she caught the sound of a horn echoing through the water, and she thought: "Ah, there he is, sailing up above—he whom I love more than my father or my mother, he who is always in my thoughts and in whose hands I would gladly place my happiness. I would venture anything to win him and an immortal soul. While my sisters are dancing away in Father's castle, I will go to the sea witch. I've always been dreadfully afraid of her, but perhaps she can help me and tell me what to do."

And so the little mermaid left her garden and set off for the place where the witch lived, on the far side of the foaming whirlpools. She had never been over there before. There were no flowers growing there and no sea grass. There was nothing but the bare, gray, sandy bottom stretching right up to the whirlpools, where the water went swirling around like roaring mill wheels and pulled everything that it could get down with it to the depths. She had to pass through the middle of those churning eddies in order to get to the domain of the sea witch. For a long stretch there was no other way than over hot, bubbling mud—the witch called it her swamp.

Now the little mermaid came to a large slimy marsh in the wood, where big, fat water snakes were rolling in the mire, showing their hideous, whitish yellow bellies. In the middle of the marsh stood a house, built with the bones of shipwrecked human folk. There sat the sea witch, letting a toad feed from her mouth, just the way people sometimes feed a canary with a piece of sugar. She called the hideous water snakes her little chicks and let them crawl all over her chest.

"I know exactly what you're after," said the sea witch. "How stupid of you! But you shall have your way, and it will bring you misfortune, my pretty princess. You want to get rid of your fish tail and in its place have a couple of stumps to walk on like a human being so that the young prince will fall in love with you and you can win an immortal soul." And with that the witch let out such a loud, repulsive laugh that the toad and the snakes fell and went sprawling on the ground. "You've come at just the right time," said the witch. "Tomorrow, once the sun is up, I would not be able to help you for another year. I shall prepare a drink for you. You will have to swim to land with it before sunrise, sit down on the shore, and swallow it. Your tail will then divide in two and shrink into what human beings call 'pretty legs.' But it will hurt. It will feel like a sharp sword passing through you. All who see you will say that you are the loveliest little human being they have ever seen. You will keep your graceful movements — no dancer will ever glide so lightly — but every step taken will make you feel as if you were treading on a sharp knife, enough to make your feet bleed. If you are prepared to endure all that, I can help you."

"Yes," said the little mermaid, and her voice trembled. But she turned her thoughts to the prince and the prize of an immortal soul.

"Think about it carefully," said the witch. "Once you take on the form of a human, you can never again be a mermaid. You won't be able to swim down through the water to your sisters and to your father's palace. The only way you can get an immortal soul is to win the prince's love and make him willing to forget his father and mother for your sake. He must have you always in his thoughts and allow the priest to join your hands to become man and wife. If the prince marries someone else, the morning thereafter your heart will break, and you will become foam on the crest of the waves."

"I'm ready," said the little mermaid, and she turned pale as death.

"But you will have to pay me," said the witch. "You're not getting my help for nothing. You have the loveliest voice of anyone who dwells down here at the bottom of the sea. You probably think that you can charm the prince with that voice, but you will have to give it to me. I am going to demand the best thing you possess as the price for my potion. You see, I have to mix in some of my own blood so that the drink will be as sharp as a double-edged sword."

"But if you take away my voice," said the little mermaid, "what will I have left?"

"Your lovely figure," said the witch, "your graceful movements, and your expressive eyes. With those you can easily enchant a human heart. . . . Well, where's your courage? Put out your little tongue and let me cut it off as my payment. Then you shall have your powerful potion."

"So be it," said the little mermaid, and the witch placed her cauldron on the fire to brew the magic potion.

"Cleanliness before everything," she said, as she scoured the vessel with a bundle of snakes she had tied together in a large knot. Then she pricked herself in the chest and let the black blood drop into the cauldron. The steam that rose created strange shapes, terrifying to behold. The witch kept tossing fresh things into the cauldron, and when the brew began to boil, it sounded like a crocodile weeping. At last the magic potion was ready, and it looked just like clear water.

"There you go," said the witch, as she cut off the little mermaid's tongue. The little mermaid was now dumb and could neither speak nor sing.

"If the polyps should seize you as you return through the wood," said the witch, "just throw a single drop of this potion on them, and their arms and fingers will be torn into a thousand pieces." But the little mermaid had no need for that. The polyps shrank back in terror when they caught sight of the glittering potion that shone in her hand like a twinkling star. And so she passed quickly through the wood, the marsh, and the roaring whirlpools.

The little mermaid could see her father's palace. The lights in the ballroom were out. Everyone there was sure to be asleep by this time. But she did not dare to go in to see them, for now she was dumb and about to leave them forever. She felt as if her heart was going to break from grief. She stole into the garden, took one flower from the beds of each of her sisters, blew a thousand kisses toward the palace, and then rose up through the dark blue waters.

The sun had not yet risen when she caught sight of the prince's palace and climbed the beautiful marble steps. The moon was shining clear and bright. The little mermaid drank the sharp, burning potion, and it seemed as if a double-edged sword was passing through her delicate body. She fainted and fell down as if dead.

The sun rose and, shining across the sea, woke her up. She felt a sharp pain. But there in front of her stood the handsome young prince. He fixed his coal-black eyes on her so earnestly that she cast down her own and realized that her fish tail was gone and that she had as pretty a pair of white legs as any young girl could wish for. But she was quite naked and so she wrapped herself in her long, flowing hair. The prince asked who she was and how she had come there, and she could only gaze back at him sweetly and sadly with her deep blue eyes, for of course she could not speak. Then he took her by the hand and led her to the palace. Every step she took, as the witch had predicted, made her feel as if she was treading on sharp knives and needles, but she willingly endured it. She walked as lightly as a bubble by the prince's side. The prince and all who saw her marveled at the beauty of her graceful movements.

She was given costly dresses of silk and muslin after she arrived. She was the most beautiful creature in the palace, but she was dumb and could neither speak nor sing. Beautiful slave girls dressed in silk and gold came out and danced before the prince and his royal parents. One sang more beautifully than all the others, and the prince clapped his hands and smiled at her. This saddened the little mermaid, for she knew that she herself could sing far more beautifully. And she thought, "Oh, if only he knew that I gave my voice away forever in order to be with him."

The slave girls then danced a graceful, gliding dance to the most enchanting music. And the little mermaid raised her lovely white arms, stood on the tips of her toes, and glided across the floor, dancing as no one had danced before. She looked more and more lovely with every step, and her eyes appealed more deeply to the heart than did the singing of the slave girls.

Everyone was enchanted, especially the prince, who called her his little foundling. She kept on dancing, even though it felt as if she were treading on sharp knives every time her foot touched the ground. The prince said that she must never leave him, and she was given permission to sleep outside his door, on a velvet cushion.

"Ah, little does he know that it was I who saved his life," thought the little mermaid. "I carried him across the sea to the temple in the woods, and I waited in the foam for someone to come and help. I saw the pretty girl that he loves better than he loves me." And the mermaid sighed deeply, for she did not know how to shed tears. "He says the girl belongs to the holy temple and that she will therefore never return to the world. They will never again meet. I am by his side, and I see him every day. I will take care of him and love him and give up my life for him."

Not long after that, there was talk that the prince would marry and that the beautiful daughter of a neighboring king would be his wife, and that was why he was rigging out a splendid ship. The prince was going to "pay a visit at a neighboring kingdom"—that was how they put it, meaning that he was going to look at his neighbor's daughter. He had a large entourage, but the little mermaid shook her head and laughed. She knew the prince's thoughts far better than anyone else.

"I shall have to go," he told her. "I have to visit this beautiful princess, because my parents insist upon it. But they cannot force me to bring her back here as my wife. I could never love her. She is not at all like the beautiful girl in the temple, whom you resemble. If I were forced to choose a bride, I would rather choose you, my dear mute foundling, with the expressive eyes." And he kissed her rosy mouth, played with her long hair, and laid his head against her heart so that it dreamed of human happiness and an immortal soul.

"You are not afraid of the sea, are you, my dear mute girl?" he asked as they stood on the deck of the splendid ship that was carrying them to the neighboring kingdom. And he told her of powerful storms and dead calms, of the strange fishes in the deep, and what divers had seen down there. She smiled at his tales, for she knew better than anyone else about the wonders at the bottom of the sea.

At night, when there was an unclouded moon and everyone was asleep but the helmsman at his wheel, the little mermaid sat by the ship's rail, gazing down through the clear water. She thought she could see her father's palace, with her old grandmother standing on top of it with the silver crown on her head, gazing through the swift current at the keel of the vessel. Then her sisters came up on the waves and looked at her with eyes full of sorrow, wringing their white hands. She beckoned to them and smiled and would have liked to tell them that she was happy and that all was going well for her. But the cabin boy came up just then, and the sisters dove down, so that the boy was sure that the white something he had seen was only foam on the water.

The next morning the ship sailed into the harbor of the neighboring king's magnificent capital. The church bells were ringing, and from the towers you could hear a flourish of trumpets. Soldiers saluted with gleaming bayonets and flying colors. Every day there was a festival. Balls and entertainments followed one another, but the princess had not yet appeared. People said that she was being brought up and educated in a holy temple, where she was learning all the royal virtues. At last she arrived.

The little mermaid was eager for a glimpse of her beauty, and she had to admit that she had never seen a more charming person. Her skin was clear and delicate, and behind long, dark eyelashes her laughing blue eyes shone with deep sincerity.

"It's you," said the prince to the princess. "You're the one who rescued me when I was lying half-dead on the beach." And he clasped his blushing bride in his arms.

"Oh, I am so very happy," he said to the little mermaid. "My dearest wish, more than I ever dared hope for, has been granted. My happiness will give you pleasure, because you're more devoted to me than anyone else." The little mermaid kissed his hand, and she felt as if her heart were already broken. The day of his wedding would mean her death, and she would turn into foam on the ocean waves.

All the church bells were ringing as the heralds rode through the streets to proclaim the betrothal. Perfumed oil was burning in precious silver lamps on every altar. The priest swung the censers, while the bride and bridegroom joined hands and received the blessing of the bishop. Dressed in silk and gold, the little mermaid stood holding the bride's train, but her ears never heard the festive music, and her eyes never saw the holy rites. She was thinking about her last night on earth and about everything that she had lost in this world.

That same evening bride and bridegroom went on board the ship. The cannon roared, the flags were waving, and in the center of the ship a sumptuous tent of purple and gold had been raised. It was strewn with luxurious cushions, for the wedded couple was to sleep there on that calm, cool night. The sails filled with the breeze, and the ship glided lightly and smoothly over the clear seas. When it grew dark, colored lanterns were lit and the sailors danced merrily on deck. The little mermaid could not help thinking of that first time she had come up from the sea and gazed on just such a scene of joyous festivities. And now she joined in the dance, swerving and swooping as lightly as a swallow that avoids pursuit. Cries of admiration greeted her from all sides. Never before had she danced so elegantly. All was joy and merriment on board until long past midnight. She laughed and danced with the others while the thought of death was in her heart. The prince kissed his lovely bride, while she played with his dark hair, and arm in arm they retired to the magnificent tent.

The ship was now hushed and quiet. Only the helmsman was there at his wheel. And the little mermaid leaned with her white arms on the rail and looked to the east for a sign of the rosy dawn. The first ray of the sun, she knew, would bring her death. Suddenly she saw her sisters rising out of the sea. They were as pale as she, but their long beautiful hair was no longer waving in the wind—it had been cut off.

"We have given our hair to the witch," they said, "to save you from the death that awaits you tonight. She has given us a knife—look, here it is. See how sharp it is? Before sunrise you must plunge it into the prince's heart.

Then, when his warm blood splashes on your feet, they will grow back together and form a fish tail, and you will be a mermaid once more. You will be able to come back down to us in the water and to live out your three hundred years before being changed into the foam of the salty sea. Make haste! Either he or you will die before sunrise. Our old grandmother has been feeling such sorrow that her white hair has been falling out, as ours fell under the witch's scissors. Kill the prince and come back to us! But make haste—look at the red streaks in the sky. In a few minutes the sun will rise, and then you will die." And with a strange deep sigh, they sank down beneath the waves.

The little mermaid drew back the purple curtain of the tent, and she saw the lovely bride sleeping with her head on the prince's chest. She bent down and kissed his handsome brow, then looked at the sky where the rosy dawn was growing brighter and brighter. She gazed at the sharp knife in her hand and again fixed her eyes on the prince, who whispered the name of his bride in his dreams—she alone was in his thoughts. The little mermaid's hand trembled as she held the knife—then she flung it far out over the waves. The water turned red where it fell, and something that looked like drops of blood came oozing out of the water. With a last glance at the prince from eyes half-dimmed in death, she threw herself from the ship into the sea and felt her body dissolve into foam.

And now the sun came rising up from the sea. Its warm and gentle rays fell on the death-chilled foam, but the little mermaid did not feel as if she were dying. She saw the bright sun and, hovering around her, hundreds of lovely creatures—she could see right through them, see the white sails of the ship and the rosy clouds in the sky. And their voice was the voice of song, yet too ethereal to be heard by mortal ears, just as no mortal eye could behold them. They had no wings, but their lightness bore them up as they floated through the air. The little mermaid saw that she had a body like theirs and that she was rising higher and higher out of the foam.

"Where am I?" she asked, and her voice sounded like that of the other beings, more ethereal than any earthly music could sound.

"Among the daughters of the air," answered the others. "A mermaid does not have an immortal soul, and she can never have one unless she wins the love of a human being. Eternity, for her, depends on a power outside her. Nor do the daughters of the air have an everlasting soul, but through good deeds they can earn one for themselves. We shall fly to the hot countries, where the stifling air of pestilence means death for humans. We shall bring cool breezes. We shall carry the fragrance of flowers through the air and send comfort and healing. When we have tried to do all the good we can in three hundred years, we shall win an immortal soul and have a share in humankind's eternal happiness. You, poor little mermaid, have tried with your whole heart to do as we are doing. You have suffered and endured and have raised yourself into the world of the spirits of the air. Now, with three hundred years of good deeds, you, too, can earn for yourself an immortal soul."

The little mermaid raised her crystal arms toward the sun, and for the first time she knew what tears felt like. On the ship there was much bustling about and sounds of life. The little mermaid saw the prince and his beautiful bride searching for her. With great sadness, they gazed at the pearly foam, as if they knew that she had thrown herself onto the waves. Unseen, she kissed the forehead of the bride, smiled at the prince, and then mounted onto a rose-red cloud that was sailing to the sky with the other children of the air.

CHAPTER 4

The Princess and the Pea

by Hans Christian Andersen

nce upon a time, there was a prince who wanted to marry a princess, but only a real princess would do. So he set off around the world to find one. There were plenty of girls who claimed to be princesses, but he could never be certain that they were really, truly princesses. There was always something that did not seem quite right: this one was too tall; that one too short; this one too stupid; that one too vain. And so he returned home, very sad indeed, for he wanted more than anything to find a real princess who could rule his kingdom with him.

One evening there was a terrible storm. There was roaring thunder and flashing lightning. The rain poured in torrents. It was a frightening storm, and in the middle of it, there was a knock at the door. The king himself went to open it and when he did, he found a princess. Or at least she said she was a princess. Her hair and clothes were soaking wet, and she was nearly blue from the cold. But, nonetheless, she insisted she was a real princess, so the king let her in.

The queen, however, wasn't so sure she was a real princess, so she ordered that a bed be prepared for the unknown guest. The servants piled twenty mattresses, one on top of the other, and then they added twenty blankets. At the very bottom of all this, the queen secretly placed a solitary pea. Then she wished the princess a good night's rest and everyone went off to sleep.

The next morning, the queen asked the princess how she had slept.

"Quite dreadfully," replied the princess. "I hardly slept a wink all night, for there was a terrible lump in my mattress. I'm black and blue all over. I don't know what it could have been."

Now the queen knew that indeed this princess was a true princess, because only a true princess could feel a pea through twenty mattresses. So the prince married the princess and ordered that the pea be placed in a royal museum. And, as far as anyone knows, it's still there today.

CHAPTER 5

Rapunzel

by The Brothers Grimm

here once was a man and a woman who wished very much to have a child. Near their cottage was a beautiful garden that belonged to a witch. One day the wife looked over the garden wall and saw a bed full of the finest lettuce. She so longed to eat it that she gave her husband no peace until he brought her some. And so he did, and the wife made a salad and ate it with great enjoyment.

In a few days, she began to long for more lettuce, and she again made her husband climb over the wall to fetch her some. He had no sooner seized a handful than he saw the witch standing beside him.

"How dare you come into my garden?" she exclaimed fiercely. "You have stolen my lettuces, and now you must pay for them. If you have a child, you will give it to me or else you will be sorry." The husband, in great fear, gave his promise.

Soon after, a little daughter was born, and the witch came and took her away. She named her Rapunzel and put her in a high tower in the forest. This tower had no stairs and no door and only one small window. When the witch visited Rapunzel, she sat beneath the window, and cried:

"Rapunzel, let down your golden hair
That I may climb it like a stair."

Rapunzel had the most beautiful long hair, and when she heard the voice of the witch, she let it hang over the windowsill right down to the ground, so that the witch could draw herself up as if it were a ladder.

When Rapunzel had grown into a beautiful maiden, it happened one day that the king's son was passing the tower and heard her singing. Her voice was so sweet that he longed to see her. The next day he came again to listen, and the next. Then he heard the witch call to Rapunzel beneath the window and saw her climb up by the maiden's long hair. The following night, when it was dark, he placed himself beneath the window and said:

"Rapunzel, let down your golden hair
That I may climb it like a stair."

Immediately the hair fell down, and he quickly climbed up and entered the tower.

Rapunzel was dreadfully frightened when she saw the prince, but she soon lost all fear. After a time, he asked her if she would marry him, and she consented.

"I will bring you a strong silk cord," said the prince, "so you can weave a ladder by which you will be able to descend from the tower. Then I will carry you to my father's castle, and we will be married."

Now the witch watched over Rapunzel very carefully, and she soon found out about the prince. She was very angry and seized poor Rapunzel's golden hair and cut it off. Then she dragged her to a lonely place in the depths of the forest and left her there.

At sunset the prince came to the tower and cried:

"Rapunzel, let down your golden hair
That I may climb it like a stair."

The witch let the hair down, and the prince climbed up to the window. What was his horror to see, instead of Rapunzel, a hideous old witch!

"Ah!" she cried, with a sneer, "you have come to carry off your bride! Rapunzel has gone away, and you will never see her again."

On hearing this, the prince was so overcome with grief that he sprang out of the window and fell among the thorn trees beneath. The thorns stuck into his eyes and blinded him, and he wandered away into the wood, lamenting and calling the name of his lost bride.

For an entire year he wandered, until at last he came to the lonely place where the witch had left Rapunzel. He heard her singing and followed the sound until, on coming near, he was clasped in her arms. When she saw that he was blind she began to weep, and two of her tears fell on his eyes and healed them. Then Rapunzel and the prince traveled back to his father's kingdom; soon afterward they were married, and lived in peace and happiness for the rest of their lives.

CHAPTER 6

Sleeping Beauty

by Charles Perrault

ong ago, in fairy times, there lived a king and queen who were very happy, having nothing to complain of but the want of children to share their joy. At last it pleased Providence to present them with a daughter. At the birth of this princess, there was great joy all over the kingdom; and at the christening seven fairies were asked to stand as godmothers, in the hope that each would offer the little princess some gift, as was always done in those days, by which means she would be adorned with every good thing that could be thought of or wished for.

The christening being over, a grand feast was prepared to entertain and thank the fairies. Before each of them was laid a splendid dish, with a spoon, a knife, and a fork of richly carved, pure gold. Just as they were going to sit down, in came a very old fairy who had not been invited. The king ordered a plate to be laid for her, but he could not give her such a case of gold as the others had, because he had had only seven made — one for each of the fairies. The aged fairy, thinking that she was slighted, muttered many threats, which were overheard by one of the fairies who sat beside her. Judging that the old fairy might give the little princess some fatal gifts, the youngest fairy hid herself behind the hangings of the room, that she might speak last and undo as much as possible the evil that the old fairy might intend.

Meanwhile the fairies began to bestow their gifts on the princess. The youngest gave her great beauty; another gave her wit; and so on with the others until the old fairy's turn came. She went forward and with a shaking head, more from spite than from age, said that the princess would have her hand pierced with a spindle, and that she would die from the wound. These awful words made the whole company tremble.

At this instant the young fairy came out from behind the curtains and spoke these words: "Be comforted, O king and queen, and be assured that your daughter shall not die of this evil. It is true that I have not power to undo what my elder has done. The princess shall indeed pierce her hand with a spindle;

but instead of dying, she shall only fall into a deep sleep, which shall last one hundred years, at the end of which a king's son will come and awaken her."

Yet the king, to turn aside the evil spoken by the old fairy, sent forth a royal order whereby every person was forbidden, on pain of death, to spin with a distaff or spindle, or even to keep them in their houses.

About fifteen years later, when the king and queen had gone on a visit to one of their summer palaces, the young princess, to amuse herself, went over the rooms of the palace and, in the gaiety of youth, climbed one of the turrets, where, in a little garret, she found an old woman spinning with a distaff. This good woman had never heard of the king's order against the spindle.

"What are you doing, Goody?" asked the princess.

"I am spinning, my pretty lass," replied the old woman, not knowing who she was.

"Oh, that is very pretty!" said the princess. "How do you do it? Give it to me, that I may try."

The old woman, to please the lady, granted her request. But the princess had no sooner taken it into her hand than, being somewhat hasty and careless, she caused the spindle to pierce her hand and she fell down in a swoon. The good old woman became alarmed and, not knowing what to do, called aloud for help. A number of servants flocked around the princess, trying every means to restore her, but all to no purpose.

And when the king returned, he remembered the prediction of the fairies, and judging very well that this must necessarily come to pass since the fairies had said it would, he had the princess carried into the finest apartment in the palace and laid upon a bed all embroidered with gold and silver. One would have taken her for a little angel, she was so very beautiful; for her swooning away had not diminished one bit of her complexion: her cheeks were carnation, and her lips like coral. She had only her eyes shut, but they heard her breathe softly, which satisfied them that she was not dead. The king commanded that they should not disturb her, but let her sleep quietly till her hour of awakening had come.

The good fairy, who had promised to save her life by causing her to sleep for one hundred years, was in the kingdom of Matakin, twelve thousand leagues off, when this accident befell the princess; but she was instantly informed of it by a dwarf who had boots with which he could tread over many leagues of ground at a stride.

The fairy left the kingdom at once and arrived at the palace about an hour later in a chariot drawn by dragons. The king handed her out of the chariot, and she approved of everything he had done; but as she had great foresight, she thought that when the princess should awake, she might be puzzled by what to do on finding herself alone in this large old palace. She therefore touched with her wand all the ladies- and gentlemen-in-waiting—in short, every person in the palace except the king and queen; she likewise touched all the horses and all the dogs down to the little spaniel that lay beside the princess on the bed.

No sooner had she done so than they all fell into a sound sleep that was to last till their mistress should awake, that they might be ready to wait upon her. All this was done in a moment, fairies never being long in doing their spiriting.

The king and queen, having kissed their child without waking her, left the palace and sent forth an order forbidding anyone to go near the spot. This, however, was needless, for in less than a quarter of an hour there sprang up all around the park such a vast number of trees, great and small bushes, briers, and brambles, twined one within the other, that neither person nor beast could pass through. Nothing could be seen but the tops of the towers of the palace, and even those only from a good way off. Indeed the fairy had given

a wonderful example of her art, in order that the princess, while she remained sleeping, might be quite secure from prying eyes.

At the end of one hundred years, the son of the king who then reigned (but not of the same family as the sleeping princess), being out hunting on that side of the country, asked what these towers were, the tops of which he saw in the midst of a great thick wood. Everyone answered according to what he had heard.

Some said it was an old ruinous castle haunted by spirits; others, that it was a place of meeting for all the witches in the land; while the most common opinion was that an ogre lived there who was in the habit of stealing all the little children he could, that he might eat them up at his leisure without anybody being able to follow him, as only he himself had the power to pass through the wood.

The prince did not know what to make of these different accounts, when an aged countryman said, "May it please Your Highness, it is about fifty years since I heard my father tell what his father had told him—that there was then in this castle a princess, the most beautiful that was ever seen; that she must sleep there for a hundred years, and would be awakened by a king's son, whose bride she would become."

The young prince felt much excited at these words and, with the hope of being himself the hero who was to end the long fairy-sleep, resolved that moment to look into it and find out how far the story might prove true. Scarcely had he advanced toward the wood when all the great trees, the bushes, and brambles gave way of their own accord to allow him to pass through.

Hurrying along the corridor

He entered a large outer courtyard, where everything he saw might have frightened anyone less brave than himself. There reigned over all a frightful silence. The image of death was everywhere present, for there was nothing to be seen but the bodies of men and animals, all seeming to be dead.

He, however, very well knew, by the jolly, rosy faces of the porters, that they were only asleep with their goblets in their hands, plainly showing that they all had fallen asleep in their cups. He then crossed a court paved with marble, went upstairs, and entered the guard chamber, where the guards were standing in their ranks with their guns upon their shoulders and snoring loudly.

After that he went through several rooms full of ladies- and gentlemen-in-waiting, some standing and others sitting, but all fast asleep.

At last he entered a chamber all gilt with gold. Here he saw upon a splendid bed, the finest sight that ever he beheld: a princess who seemed to be about fifteen years of age, and whose rare beauty had in it something divine. He went near with fear and trembling, and could not keep from bending his knee before her.

Now the trance was at an end. The princess awoke and looked on him with eyes more tender than the first view would seem to admit. "Is it you, my prince? How long I've been waiting for you!" The prince, charmed with these words and the manner in which they were spoken, assured her that he loved her far better than himself.

Their meeting was so quiet that indeed they wept more than they talked. He was more at a loss for words than she was, and little wonder, as she had had time to think on what to say to him; for it was very probable, though the history mentions nothing of it, that the good fairy during so long a sleep had given her pleasant dreams. In short, they talked for about four hours together and yet said not half of what they had to say.

In the meantime, the people of the palace, having awakened at the same time as the princess, each began to perform their duties; and as they were not all in love like their mistress, but were rather ready to die with hunger, the ladies-in-waiting grew very impatient and told the princess that supper was served. The prince helped the princess to rise, for she was already dressed in splendid robes, though His Royal Highness did not tell her that her clothes were cut on the pattern of those of his great-grandmother, which were long out of fashion. However, she looked no less beautiful than if her dress had been more modern.

They went into the great hall of looking glasses, where they supped to the sound of delightful music. With fiddles and spinet, tunes a century old were played. After supper the chaplain joined the happy pair in wedlock.

The next day they left the old castle and returned to court, where the king was delighted to welcome back the prince with his lovely bride, who was thenceforth known, both by her own people and by those who handed down the story to us, as the "Sleeping Beauty of the Wood."

CHAPTER 7

Snow White and the Seven Dwarfs

by The Brothers Grimm

nce upon a time, in the middle of winter, when the flakes of snow fell like feathers from the sky, a queen sat at a window set in an ebony frame and sewed. While she was sewing and watching the snowfall, she pricked her finger with her needle, and three drops of blood dropped on the snow. And because the crimson looked so beautiful on the white snow, she thought, "Oh that I had a child as white as snow, as red as blood, and as black as the wood of this ebony frame!"

Soon afterward she had a little daughter, who had skin as white as snow, lips as red as blood, and hair as black as ebony. She was named Snow White. But when the child was born, the queen died.

After a year had gone by, the king took another wife. She was a handsome lady but proud and haughty, and could not endure that anyone should surpass her in beauty. She had a wonderful mirror, and whenever she walked up to it and looked at herself in it, she said:

"Little glass upon the wall,
Who is fairest of us all?"

Then the mirror replied:

"Lady queen, so grand and tall,
Thou art the fairest of them all."

And she was satisfied, for she knew the mirror always told the truth. But Snow White grew ever taller and fairer, and at seven years old was beautiful as the day, and more beautiful than the queen herself. So once, when the queen asked of her mirror:

"Little glass upon the wall,
Who is fairest of us all?"

It answered:

"Lady queen, you are grand and tall,
But Snow White is fairest of you all."

Then the queen was startled, and turned yellow and green with envy. From that hour she so hated Snow White that she burned with secret wrath whenever she saw the maiden. Pride and envy grew apace like weeds in her heart, till she had no rest day or night.

So she called a huntsman and said, "Take the child out in the forest, for I will endure her no longer in my sight. Kill her and bring me her heart as a token that you have done it."

The huntsman obeyed and led the child away; but when he had drawn his hunting knife, and was about to pierce Snow White's innocent heart, she began to weep and said, "Ah! Dear huntsman, spare my life, and I will run deep into the wild forest and never more come home."

The huntsman took pity on her because she looked so lovely and said, "Run away then, poor child!"

"The wild beasts will soon make an end of thee," he thought; but it seemed as if a stone had been rolled from his heart because he had avoided taking her life; and as a little bear came by just then, he killed it, took out its heart, and carried it as a token to the queen. She made the cook dress it with salt, and then the wicked woman ate it and thought she had eaten Snow White's heart.

The poor child was now all alone in the great forest, and she felt frightened as she looked at all the leafy trees, and knew not what to do. So she began to run, and ran over the sharp stones and through the thorns; and the wild beasts passed close to her but did her no harm. She ran as long as her feet could carry her, and when evening closed in, she saw a little house and ran toward it to rest herself.

Everything in the house was very small, but I cannot tell you how pretty and clean it was. There stood a little table, covered with a white tablecloth, on which were seven little plates (each little plate with its own little spoon), also seven little knives and forks, and seven little cups. Around the walls stood seven little beds close together, with sheets as white as snow. Snow White, being so hungry and thirsty, ate a little of the vegetables and bread on each plate, and drank a drop of wine from every cup, for she did not like to empty one entirely.

Then, being very tired, she laid herself down on one of the beds but could not make herself comfortable, for one was too long and another too short. The seventh, luckily, was just right; so there she stayed, said her prayers, and fell asleep.

When it had grown quite dark, home came the masters of the house, seven dwarfs, who delved and mined for iron in the mountains. They lighted their seven candles, and as soon as there was a light in the kitchen, they saw that someone had been there, for it was not quite so orderly as they had left it.

The first said, "Who has been sitting on my stool?" The second, "Who has eaten off my plate?" The third, "Who has taken part of my loaf?" The fourth, "Who has touched my vegetables?" The fifth, "Who has used my fork?" The sixth, "Who has cut with my knife?" The seventh, "Who has drunk out of my little cup?"

Then the first dwarf looked about and saw that there was a slight hollow in his bed, so he asked, "Who has been lying in my little bed?"

The others came running, and each called out, "Someone has also been lying in my bed!" But the seventh, when he looked at his bed, saw Snow White there, fast asleep. He called the others, who flocked around with cries of surprise, fetched their candles, and cast the light on Snow White.

"Oh, heaven!" they cried. "What a lovely child!" and were so pleased that they would not wake her, but let her sleep on in the little bed. The seventh dwarf slept with all his companions in turn, an hour with each, and so they spent the night.

When it was morning, Snow White woke up and was frightened when she saw the seven dwarfs. They were friendly, however, and inquired her name.

"Snow White," answered she.

"How have you found your way to our house?" asked the dwarfs.

So she told them how her stepmother had tried to kill her, how the huntsman had spared her life, and how she had run the whole day through, till at last she had found their little house.

Then the dwarfs said, "If thou wilt keep our house, cook, make our beds, wash, sew and knit, and make all neat and clean, thou canst stay with us, and shalt want for nothing."

"I will, right willingly," said Snow White. So she dwelt with them, and kept their house in order. For a time they knew great happiness.

Every morning they went out among the mountains to seek iron and gold, and came home ready for supper in the evening.

The maiden being left alone all day long, the good dwarfs warned her, saying, "Beware of thy wicked stepmother, who will soon find out that thou art here; take care that thou lettest nobody in."

The queen, however, after having, as she thought, eaten Snow White's heart, had no doubt that she was again the first and fairest woman in the world; so she walked up to her mirror and said:

"Little glass upon the wall,
Who is fairest of us all?"

The mirror replied:

"Lady queen, so grand and tall,
Here, you are fairest of them all;
But over the hills, with the seven dwarfs old,
Lives Snow White, fairer a hundredfold."

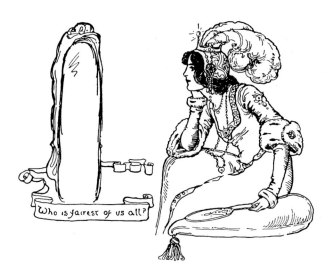

Who is fairest of us all?

She trembled, knowing the mirror never told a falsehood; she felt sure that the huntsman had deceived her and that Snow White was still alive. She pondered once more, late and early, early and late, how best to kill Snow White—for envy gave her no rest, day or night, while she herself was not the fairest lady in the land.

When she had planned what to do, she painted her face, dressed herself like an old peddler woman, and altered her appearance so much that no one could have known her. In this disguise she went over the seven hills to where the seven dwarfs dwelt, knocked at the door, and cried, "Good wares, cheap! Very cheap!"

Snow White looked out of the window and cried, "Good morning, good woman. What have you to sell?"

"Good wares, smart wares," answered the queen, "laces of all colors"; and she drew out one that was woven of colored silk.

"I may surely let this honest dame in!" thought Snow White; so she unfastened the door and bought for herself the pretty lace.

"Child," said the old woman, "what a figure thou art! Let me lace thee properly for once." Snow White feared no harm, so stepped in front of her and allowed her bodice to be fastened up with the new lace.

But the old woman laced so quick and laced so tight that Snow White's breath was stopped and she fell down as if dead. "Now I am fairest at last," said the old woman to herself and sped away.

The seven dwarfs came home soon after, at eventide, but how alarmed they were to find their poor Snow White lifeless on the ground! They lifted her up into bed and, seeing that she was laced too tightly, cut the lace of her bodice; she began to breathe faintly and slowly returned to life. When the dwarfs heard what had happened, they said, "The old peddler woman was none other than the wicked queen. Be careful of thyself, and open the door to no one if we are not at home."

The cruel stepmother walked up to her mirror when she reached home and said:

"Little glass upon the wall,
Who is fairest of us all?"

To which it answered, as it had before:

"Lady queen, so grand and tall,
Here, you are fairest of them all;
But over the hills, with the seven dwarfs old,
Lives Snow White, fairer a hundredfold."

When she heard this, she was so alarmed that all the blood rushed to her heart, for she saw plainly that Snow White was still alive.

"This time," said she, "I will think of some means that shall destroy her utterly," and with the help of witchcraft, in which she was skillful, she made a poisoned comb. Then she changed her dress and took the shape of another old woman.

Again she crossed the seven hills to the home of the seven dwarfs, knocked at the door, and cried, "Good wares, very cheap!"

Snow White looked out and said, "Go away! I dare let no one in."

"You may surely be allowed to look!" answered the old woman, and she drew out the poisoned comb and held it up. The girl was so pleased with it that she let herself be cajoled and opened the door.

When the bargain was struck, the dame said, "Now let me dress your hair properly for once." Poor Snow White took no heed, and let the old woman begin; but the comb had scarcely touched her hair before the poison worked, and she fell down senseless.

"Paragon of beauty!" said the wicked woman, "all is over with thee now," and she went away.

Luckily, it was near evening, and the seven dwarfs soon came home. When they found Snow White lifeless on the ground, they at once suspected her stepmother. They searched, and found the poisoned comb; and as soon as they had drawn it out, Snow White came to herself and told them what had happened. Again they warned her to be careful and open the door to no one.

The queen placed herself before the mirror at home and said:

"Little glass upon the wall,
Who is fairest of us all?"

But it again answered:

"Lady queen, so grand and tall,
Here, you are fairest of them all;
But over the hills, with the seven dwarfs old,
Lives Snow White, fairer a hundredfold."

When she heard the mirror speak thus, she quivered with rage. "Snow White shall die," she cried, "if it costs my own life!"

Then she went to a secret and lonely chamber, where no one ever disturbed her, and compounded an apple of deadly poison. Ripe and rosy-cheeked, it was so beautiful to look upon that all who saw it longed for it, but it would bring death to any who should eat it. When the apple was ready, she painted her face, disguised herself as a peasant woman and journeyed over the seven hills to where the seven dwarfs dwelt.

At the sound of the knock, Snow White put her head out of the window and said, "I cannot open the door to anybody, for the seven dwarfs have forbidden me to do so."

"Very well," replied the peasant woman. "I only want to be rid of my apples. Here I will give you one of them!"

"No!" said Snow White. "I dare not take it."

"Art thou afraid of being poisoned?" asked the old woman. "Look here; I will cut the apple in two, and you shall eat the rosy side, and I the white."

Now the fruit was so cunningly made, that only the rosy side was poisoned. Snow White longed for the pretty apple, and when she saw the peasant woman eating it, she could resist no longer, but stretched out her hand and took the poisoned half. She had scarcely tasted it when she fell lifeless to the ground.

The queen, laughing loudly, watched her with a barbarous look and cried, "O thou who art white as snow, red as blood, and black as ebony, the seven dwarfs cannot awaken thee this time!"

And when she asked the mirror at home:

"Little glass upon the wall,
Who is fairest of us all?"

the mirror at last replied:

"Lady queen, so grand and tall,
You are fairest of them all."

So her envious heart had as much repose as an envious heart can ever know.

When the dwarfs came home in the evening, they found Snow White lying breathless and motionless on the ground. They lifted her up, searched whether she had anything poisonous about her, unlaced her, combed her hair, and washed her with water and wine; but all was useless, for they could not bring the darling back to life. They laid her on a bier, and all the seven placed themselves around it and mourned for her three long days.

Then they would have buried her, but that she still looked so fresh and lifelike and had such lovely rosy cheeks. "We cannot lower her into the dark earth," they said; and they caused a transparent coffin of glass to be made, so that she could be seen on all sides, and laid her in it, writing her name outside in letters of gold, which told that she was the daughter of a king.

Then they placed the coffin on the mountain above, and one of them always stayed by it and guarded it. But there was little need to guard it, for even the wild animals came and mourned for Snow White. The birds likewise, first an owl, and then a raven, and afterward a dove.

Long, long years did Snow White lie in her coffin unchanged, looking as though asleep, for she was still white as snow, red as blood, and her hair was black as ebony.

At last the son of a king chanced to wander into the forest, and came to the dwarfs' house for a night's shelter. He saw the coffin on the mountain with the beautiful Snow White in it, and read what was written there in letters of gold. Then he said to the dwarfs, "Let me have the coffin! I will give you whatever you'd like to ask for it."

But the dwarfs answered, "We would not part with it for all the gold in the world."

He said again, "Yet give it me; for I cannot live without seeing Snow White, and though she is dead, I will prize and honor her as my beloved."

Then the good dwarfs took pity on him and gave him the coffin.

The prince had it borne away by his servants. They happened to stumble over a bush, and the shock forced the bit of poisoned apple that Snow White had tasted out of her throat. Immediately she opened her eyes, raised the coffin lid, and sat up alive once more. "Oh, heaven!" cried she. "Where am I?"

The prince answered joyfully, "Thou art with me," and told her what had happened, saying, "I love thee more dearly than anything else in the world. Come with me to my father's castle and be my wife."

Snow White, well pleased, went with him, and they were married with much state and grandeur.

The wicked stepmother was invited to the feast. Richly dressed, she stood before the mirror and asked of it:

"Little glass upon the wall,
Who is fairest of us all?"

The mirror answered:

"Lady queen, so grand and tall,
Here, you are fairest of them all;
But the young queen over the mountains old,
Is fairer than you a thousandfold."

The evil-hearted woman uttered a curse and could scarcely endure her anguish. She first resolved not to attend the wedding, but curiosity would not allow her to rest. She determined to travel and see who that young queen could be, who was the most beautiful in all the world. When she arrived and found that it was Snow White alive again, she stood petrified with terror and despair.

Then two iron shoes, heated burning hot, were drawn out of the fire with a pair of tongs and laid before her feet. She was asked either to put them on, and to go and dance at Snow White's wedding—or to leave and nevermore be seen.

CHAPTER 8

Beauty and the Beast

by Madame Marie Leprince de Beaumont

here once lived a merchant who owned a great fleet of ships. He was proud of those ships, but prouder yet of his daughters. The eldest was fair, the second even more so, but the youngest was so lovely that people called her "Beauty."

One year, a great tempest scattered the merchant's ships. Thus, the merchant went from being very rich to being very poor. He sold his mansion and went to live in a tiny cottage. The two elder sisters did not meet with this sudden change of fortune bravely, but Beauty ignored her own troubles and set out to help her father. She did all the work of the cottage and was always merry. It seemed that her name suited her better every day.

At last, news came that one of the ships had cast anchor in a distant seaport and the merchant was summoned to claim it. He called his daughters to him and said, "Dear children, we shall never be rich again, but perhaps we may be a bit less poor. I do not want to return to you empty-handed, so choose what you would like me to bring you." The eldest asked for a string of pearls; the second for a pair of ruby earrings.

"And I," said Beauty, "would like a rose plant for my garden."

When he reached the seaport, the merchant learned that the ship had been almost completely ruined, so he could only afford to buy wooden beads and glass earrings for his daughters.

"Luckily," he said to himself, "I shall not have to disappoint Beauty. It should be no hard matter to find a rosebush." But he soon found that it was a very hard matter indeed. He could have tulips and lilies by the dozen, but not a rose could be found.

"Alas," said the merchant, "I shall have to disappoint my Beauty after all."

The road home wound through a dark forest. Toward nightfall, the merchant began to realize that he had lost his way. Where he had expected to find an inn, he found only tangled trees. Still, he pushed ahead and soon he saw a twinkling of light.

It was not long before he reached the gates of a house. The gates were ajar, so he led his horse up the drive. Though he shouted at the top of his voice, no one answered. The door was open, and the merchant could see that lamps were lit and a bright fire burned in the hearth. The merchant hesitated, but it was growing late, so he decided to tether his horse and sit by the fire until someone should appear.

When he returned from the stable, he was amazed to see that a tempting supper had been set forth. Again he hesitated, but he was very hungry and the supper smelled very good, so he sat down and enjoyed the meal. After supper, the merchant began to feel sleepy. Through the half-open door he could see a bed. He lay down and by the time he woke up, the sun was shining and breakfast had been laid in the hall. Full of astonishment, the merchant ate. Then he went to fetch his horse, which he found groomed and saddled. He led his horse down the drive, calling thanks for all the kindness he had received. Just as he was about to ride away, he caught sight of a magnificent rosebush. Remembering his promise to Beauty, he decided to cut just one flower. But no sooner had his knife touched the rose than he heard a terrible roar and a most fearsome-looking creature appeared.

"Is this your gratitude?" asked the Beast "I treated you as an honored guest, and you repay me by stealing that which I love more than anything else."

"Sir," said the poor merchant, trembling, "if I had known, I would not have laid a finger on the rose. But I promised my daughter a rose and I did not want to disappoint her."

"You love your daughter very much then?" asked the Beast.

"Truly, sir, I do," answered the merchant. "She is not only beautiful, but she has the kindest heart in the world."

"Hmm," growled the Beast, "I will let you go, provided that you promise me that within seven days you will either return or send this daughter of yours in your stead."

The poor merchant sorrowfully gave his word.

"Take the rose," said the Beast, "and this bag of gold. In seven days I shall be standing here. Woe to you and yours, if neither you nor your daughter should come by that day."

When the merchant reached home, his daughters ran out to meet him. The two elder ones jumped for joy when they saw the bags of gold dangling from the saddle, but their joy turned to sadness when they heard of his strange adventure.

"Do not weep, my children," said the merchant. "I ought not to have touched those roses."

"Dearest father," whispered Beauty, "it was my fault. I will go in your place."

"Never!" cried her father.

"I will go," repeated Beauty. "Perhaps the Beast will not kill me. Poor Beast. He must be very sad."

Nothing that her father or her sisters could say would change Beauty's mind. When the seventh day came, she kissed them all farewell and set off on her journey.

Though the Beast had said that he would be waiting at the gate, Beauty saw nobody when she arrived. She led her horse into the stable and then tiptoed into the house, dreading at every moment to see the fearsome face of the Beast.

She was surprised to find a door marked "Beauty's Room." When she opened it she found herself in a lovely room filled with tapestries. There was a silver cage full of bullfinches and canaries in one corner and a golden harp in another, and in the center stood a rosebush in a great bronze pot.

"It seems," thought Beauty, "that I am not to be gobbled up after all!"

In one of the outer rooms, she found a dainty supper laid for one. "I suppose," she thought, "the poor Beast always has to eat alone."

Hardly had she finished her supper, when the door opened and the Beast came slowly into the room. Beauty uttered a cry, for he really was a fearsome Beast. But she soon saw that she had no reason to fear, for the expression on his shaggy face was sad rather than fierce.

"You are afraid of me," said the Beast, in a gruff voice.

"Not now," returned Beauty, gently.

"Are you willing," asked the Beast, "to spend a year in this house, to save your father? If the sight of me is terrible to you, I can look at you from a distance. That will be enough for me."

The next day when Beauty was in the garden, she caught sight of the Beast hidden among the trees. He looked so sad that she called out, "Sir Beast, I have something I wish to say to you!"

The Beast came eagerly forward. "I am afraid that I must have hurt you last night," said Beauty, "when I agreed to stay here only if you kept out of my sight. Perhaps you would like to come and talk to me sometimes when I walk in the garden."

"I should like it very much," returned the Beast. "I never have anybody to talk to."

A week passed, and every morning Beauty and the Beast strolled about the garden. Beauty was surprised to find that her host could be a most interesting companion.

"Were you playing the harp last night, Beauty?" the Beast asked one morning.

"Yes," said Beauty, "but I soon got tired of playing as there was no one to listen."

"May I listen outside the door?" asked the Beast.

"Of course you may," said Beauty.

The next day when she began to play, she heard footsteps outside the door and called out, "You could hear better if you came in, Sir Beast!" So the Beast came in, looking so delighted that for a moment she almost forgot he was a Beast at all.

After a little while, Beauty began to wonder how her father and sisters were. The Beast soon saw that she was fretting. When she told him why, he brought her a round bronze mirror. "This mirror," he said, "will tell you what you want to know."

Beauty gazed into the mirror, and there she saw her father weeping. As the days passed, Beauty became more and more anxious about her father. At last the Beast said to her, "Dear Beauty, I will not keep you here when your heart is elsewhere. You can go whenever you wish."

"Can I go tomorrow?" asked Beauty.

"Today, if you wish," returned the Beast.

But he spoke so sadly that she said, "Tomorrow will be soon enough."

When she said these words, two tears gathered in the Beast's eyes and rolled down his shaggy cheeks.

"I love you so, dear Beauty," said the Beast, "that when you leave my heart will break. But I love you too much to keep you here, where you must be very unhappy."

"Not so," answered Beauty, gently. "I have spent many happy hours here with you, Sir Beast, and I shall often remember them. But my father is so sad without me, that I must go to him."

"That is very natural," sighed the Beast.

The next morning when Beauty set off for home, she was surprised that the Beast did not come out to bid her good-bye. The poor beast was, in truth, too heartbroken. But he watched her from a distance and saw her wave farewell to the garden before she passed through the iron gates and disappeared from sight.

The merchant and his two elder daughters were greatly astonished when Beauty returned. Hardly had she begun to tell her story, when four men arrived with a huge leather trunk. On the lid was a label: "To Beauty, from the Beast." The sisters uttered loud cries of delight when they saw what treasures were within. At the very bottom of the heap lay the bronze mirror.

"I will hang that on the wall of my room," said Beauty.

For a few days Beauty was so glad to be home again that she almost forgot about the Beast. But soon she began to think about him. Tunes that she used to play to him on the harp would come suddenly into her mind, or when she began to read a book she would remember that the Beast had read it and had told her about it. Then one day she suddenly remembered the mirror. She ran upstairs and took it down from the wall. In it she saw a corner of the Beast's garden. The Beast was lying on the grass weeping.

"My poor Beast!" cried Beauty.

She slipped away, saddled her horse, and galloped until she reached the Beast's house. Then she ran from room to room, calling him, but all was silent. So Beauty ran to the garden. There she found the poor beast lying, almost lifeless. At the sound of Beauty's voice, the Beast tried to rise, but he was too weak. So she knelt beside him and lifted his shaggy head on her arm. Then he opened his eyes and said faintly, "Beauty, why have you come back to me?"

"Because I love you," said Beauty.

She bent to kiss him. But even though she loved him, she had to shut her eyes, because he was so fearful to behold.

"Look at me, dear Beauty," said the Beast.

Beauty opened her eyes and saw that he was a beast no longer.

"Dear Beauty," he said. "I was doomed by a wicked fairy to wear the mask of a monster and to live a life of sorrow and loneliness until someone should love me despite my terrible looks. Only by a kiss could I be freed. Your compassion has broken the spell."

When the merchant received a letter from Beauty bidding him to receive her and her husband, he was much astonished and a little alarmed. His elder daughters screamed at the very idea of receiving a beast as a brother-in-law.

You can just imagine their surprise and delight when they found that he was not such a beast after all! In fact, they were charmed to find that he was a handsome prince and their sister his lovely bride.

~ Acknowledgments ~

We wish to thank the following properties whose cooperation has made this unique collection possible. All care has been taken to trace ownership of these selections and to make a full acknowledgment. If any errors or omissions have occurred, they will be corrected in subsequent editions, provided notification is sent to the compiler.

Front Cover	Margaret Tarrant. From *Fairy Tales*, n.d.
Front Flap	Anonymous. From *The Ideal Fairy Book*, n.d.
Endpapers	Warwick Gobel. From *The Fairy Book*, 1913.
Half-title Page	E. V. B. From *Beauty and the Beast*, n.d.
Frontispiece	Maxfield Parrish. *Cinderella*, 1914.
Title Page	Eulalie. From *Fairy Tales That Never Grow Old*, 1923.
Copyright Page	Jennie Harbour. From *My Book of Favorite Fairy Tales*, n.d.
Preface	W. Heath Robinson. From *Hans Andersen's Fairy Tales*, 1913.
10	Hedvig Collin. From *The Princess and the Pea*, n.d.
11	Millicent Sowerby. From *Cinderella*, n.d.
12	A. L. Bowley. From *Old Fairy Tales*, n.d.
13	Anonymous. From *The Ideal Fairy Book*, n.d.
14	Arthur Rackham. From *Cinderella*, 1919.
15	E. S. Hardy. From *Mother Goose Nursery Tales*, n.d.
17	Frank Adams. From *Favorite Nursery Tales*, n.d.
18	Jennie Harbour. From *My Book of Favorite Fairy Tales*, n.d.
19	W. Gunston. From *Cinderella*, 1876.
21	Charles Robinson. From *The Big Book of Fairy Tales*, n.d.
22	Margaret Evans Price. From *Once Upon a Time*, 1921.
23	Anonymous. From *Cinderella*, circa 1900.
24	Anonymous. From *Stories Children Love*, 1927.
25	Jennie Harbour. From *My Book of Favorite Fairy Tales*, n.d.
26	Elenore Abbott. From *Grimm's Fairy Tales*, 1921.
27	Margaret Evans Price. From *Once Upon a Time*, 1921.

28   Anonymous. From *Cinderella,* circa 1900.

29   Millicent Sowerby. From *Cinderella,* n.d.

30   Honor Appleton. From *A Treasury of Tales for Little Folks,* 1927.

31   E. S. Hardy. From *Mother Goose Nursery Tales,* n.d.

32   Warwick Goble. From *The Fairy Book,* 1913.

33   Anonymous. From *The Ideal Fairy Book,* n.d.

34   Anonymous. From *Favourite Tales of the Nursery,* 1894.

35   Edmund Dulac. From *The Sleeping Beauty and Other Fairy Tales,* n.d.

36   Anonymous. From *Past Pleasures,* circa 1820.

37   Anonymous. From *The Story Teller,* 1902.

38   E. S. Hardy. From *My Nursery Tale Book,* n.d.

39   Walter Crane. From *Cinderella,* n.d.

40   Mabel Lucie Attwell. From *The Frog Prince,* n.d.

41   Walter Crane. From *Household Stories by the Brothers Grimm,* n.d.

42   Walter Crane. From *The Frog Prince,* n.d.

43   W. H. Margetson. From *The Old Fairy Tales,* n.d.

44   Eulalie. From *Fairy Tales That Never Grow Old,* 1923.

45   Anonymous. From *The Story Teller,* 1902.

46   E. S. Hardy. From *Stories from Hans Andersen,* n.d.

47   Arthur Rackham. From *Fairy Tales by Hans Andersen,* 1932.

48   Frank C. Papé. From *Hans Andersen's Fairy Tales,* 1919.

49   Margaret Tarrant. From *Fairy Stories from Hans Christian Andersen,* n.d.

50–51   Louis Rhead. From *Hans Andersen's Fairy Tales,* 1914.

52   Charles Robinson. From *Fairy Tales from Hans Christian Andersen,* 1899.

54   Margaret Tarrant. From *Fairy Stories from Hans Christian Andersen,* n.d.

55   W. Heath Robinson. From *Hans Andersen's Fairy Tales,* 1913.

56   Margaret Tarrant. From *Fairy Stories from Hans Christian Andersen,* n.d.

57   Helen Stratton. From *The Fairy Tales of Hans Christian Andersen,* 1899.

58   Jennie Harbour. From *The Little Mermaid,* 1932.

60   Helen Stratton. From *The Fairy Tales of Hans Christian Andersen,* 1899.

62   Margaret Tarrant. From *Fairy Stories from Hans Christian Andersen,* n.d.

63   V. Pedersen. From *Wonder Stories Told for Children,* 1883.

64   E. S. Hardy. From *Stories from
            Hans Andersen,* n.d.

67   Helen Stratton. From *The Fairy Tales of
            Hans Christian Andersen,* 1899.

68   Cecile Walton. From *Hans Andersen's
            Fairy Tales,* 1911.

69 (top)   Anne Anderson. From *Andersen's
            Fairy Stories,* n.d.

69 (bottom) Helen Stratton. From *The Fairy Tales
            of Hans Christian Andersen,* 1899.

70   Edmund Dulac. From *Stories from
            Hans Andersen,* 1911.

71   W. Heath Robinson. From *Hans Andersen's Fairy Tales*, 1913.

72   Kay Nielsen. From *Hansel and Gretel*, 1925.

73   Hedvig Collin. From *The Princess and the Pea*, n.d.

74   Kay Nielsen. From *Hansel and Gretel*, 1925.

75   Hedvig Collin. From *The Princess and the Pea*, n.d.

77   Anne Anderson. From *Grimm's Fairy Tales*, n.d.

78   Walter Crane. From *Household Stories from the Brothers Grimm*, 1924.

79   Anonymous. From *The Favorite Book of Nursery Tales*, 1893.

80   Margaret Tarrant. From *Favorite Fairy Tales*, n.d.

81   Anonymous. From *The Ideal Fairy Book*, n.d.

82   Edmund Dulac. From *The Sleeping Beauty and Other Fairy Tales*, n.d.

83   Anonymous. From *The Ideal Fairy Book*, n.d.

84   Anonymous. From *The Ideal Fairy Book*, n.d.

85   Honor Appleton. From *Perrault's Fairy Tales*, n.d.

86   Charles Robinson. From *The Big Book of Fairy Tales*, n.d.

87   Arthur Rackham. From *The Fairy Tales of the Brothers Grimm*, 1909.

88   Arthur Rackham. From *The Fairy Tales of the Brothers Grimm*, 1909.

89   Charles Folkard. From *Grimm's Fairy Tales*, 1911.

90   Anonymous. From *The Favorite Book of Nursery Tales*, 1893.

91   Jennie Harbour. From *My Book of Favorite Fairy Tales*, n.d.

92   Kay Nielsen. From *Hansel and Gretel*, 1925.

93   Jesse Wilcox Smith. From *A Child's Book of Stories*, 1919.

94   Anonymous. From *The World's Best Fairy Stories*, 1911.

95   Walter Crane. From *Household Stories by the Brothers Grimm*, 1886.

96   Innes Fripp. From *The Old Fairy Tales*, n.d.

97   Charles Robinson. From *The True Annals of Fairy Land*, n.d.

98   Walter Crane. From *Household Stories by the Brothers Grimm*, 1886.

99   W. H. Margetson. From *The Old Fairy Tales*, n.d.

100   E. S. Hardy. From *My Nursery Tale Book*, n.d.

101   O. Kubel. From a German postcard, n.d.

102   John Hassall. From *Popular Nursery Stories*, n.d.

103   E. S. Hardy. From *My Nursery Tale Book*, n.d.

104   Anonymous. *Snow White at the Seven Dwarfs' Cottage*, n.d.

105   John Hassall. From *Popular Nursery Stories*, n.d.

106   Margaret Tarrant. From *Fairy Tales*, n.d.

107   Paul Menerheim. From *Kinder und Hausmarchen*, 1895.

108   Arthur Rackham. From *The Fairy Tales of the Brothers Grimm*, 1909.

109   Millicent Sowerby. From *Grimm's Fairy Tales*, 1909.

110   Anonymous. From *My Nursery Tale Book*, n.d.

111   Anonymous. From *The Old Fairy Tales*, n.d.

112   Arthur Rackham. From *The Fairy Tales of the Brothers Grimm*, 1909.

114   Anonymous. From *Fairy Land Stories*, 1909.

115   A. H. Watson. From *Told Again*, 1927.

116   O. Kubel. From a German postcard, n.d.

117   Bess Livings. From *Snow White and the Seven Dwarfs*, n.d.

118   W. C. Drupsteen. From *Snowdrop*, n.d.

119   Lancelot Speed. From *The Red Fairy Book*, 1890.

120   Edmund Dulac. From *The Sleeping Beauty and
          Other Fairy Tales*, 1910.

121   E. S. Hardy. From *My Nursery Book*, n.d.

123   Walter Crane. From *Goody Two Shoes' Picture Book*, n.d.

124   A. L. Bowley. From *Beauty and the Beast*, n.d.

125   Margaret Evans Price. From *Once Upon a Time*, 1921.

126   A. L. Bowley. From *Beauty and the Beast*, n.d.

128   Warwick Gobel. From *The Fairy Book*, 1913.

129   Margaret Evans Price. From *Once Upon a Time*, 1921.

130   Walter Crane. From *Household Stories by the Brothers
          Grimm*, 1924.

131   Arthur Rackham. From *Cinderella*, 1919

132   Herm Vogel. From *Kinder and Hausmarchen*, n.d.

133   F. Stibbert. *Rapunzel's Wedding Gown*, 1914

Back Flap Jennie Harbour. From *My Book of Favorite
           Fairy Tales*, n.d.

Back Cover W. H. Margetson. From *Stories from Grimm*, n.d.